"That is i screamed, slamming his fist against a stone column. "There is always a Keeper of the Book!"

"And where is the Book now?" Rainna asked. "It has been removed from the castle sanctuary."

"I can assure you princess, that the Book is safely in my care," Murlox said. "Here in the castle."

"I wish to see it," she said.

"You shall witness its destruction soon enough," Murlox replied.

"There is no power in this realm that can destroy the ancient Book," Rainna remarked. "No matter how many armies you bring, no matter how long you oppress the people, there will come a time when the righteousness of the King will return to this land led by the courage of his Knights. You know it. You feel it. The time is coming. Soon."

The Golden Knight #1
The Boy Is Summoned

Happy Reading!

Justin Clark

The Golden Knight #1
The Boy Is Summoned

By
Steve Clark and **Justin Clark**

Based on Characters Created
by **Justin Clark**

Illustrations
by **Taylor Gibson**

**New Horizons Press, an imprint of
That Guy Media, LLC.**
United States of America

This is a work of fiction. All of the characters, organizations, and events portrayed in this story are either products of the authors' imaginations or are used fictitiously.

This book is being published in paperback by New Horizons Press, an imprint of That Guy Media, LLC.

ISBN 978-0-9647933-9-2

Published by New Horizons Press, an imprint of That Guy Media, LLC.
New Horizons Press, an imprint of That Guy Media, LLC and associated logos are trademarks and/or registered trademarks of New Horizons Press, an imprint of That Guy Media, LLC.

Printed in the United States of America

10 9 8 7 6 5 4 3 2 1

To my wife, Leslie, who first gave me the dream - S.C.

To my art teacher, Mrs. Phyllis Bickford, and my social studies teacher, Ms. Gin Thompson, for their inspiration to always follow my dreams- J.C.

In The Beginning....

And this is how the Great Divide came to be. Once there was one Kingdom and the King ruled over his people with a just and fair law. The Law came from the ancient Book. Many had written the Law into the Book, but all of the Law came from the King. Through the Book and the King, the people prospered and there was peace throughout the land.

But in those days, there came Flar, the evil fire lord, who promised the people an easy way to an even better life. To gain this, they would only need to turn away from the Law of the Book and the King. The people were fooled by the empty promises of Flar and fearful of his armies.

In the Great Battle, the people betrayed the King and his winged avengers. To save the Kingdom, the King created the Great Divide, a wall of supernatural energy, which separates the Kingdom

from the people. The Book remains in the hands of Flar, who seeks to destroy it and all of its wisdom and power. Only through the Book can a person cross the Great Divide and regain the Kingdom.

So the people have suffered under the harsh rule of Flar, the evil fire lord. They long to open the Book and enter into the Kingdom once again.

And the people still remember the legends of the heroic Knights, defenders of the Kingdom and guardians of the people. Knights of courage and virtue who performed great deeds in the name of the King.

So it has been for countless generations...

Chapter One

The King stood on the castle walls staring out at the energy barrier known as the Great Divide. Marsonee, the archangel, dressed in full battle armor, approached the King from behind through a stone door. As Marsonee drew near, he knelt down on one knee.

"You summoned me, my King?" Marsonee calmly asked.

The King turned and smiled at his winged friend. He extended his hand. "Arise," he said.

"As you wish," Marsonee replied, rising to his feet.

"It is time," the King remarked, turning back to face the Great Divide.

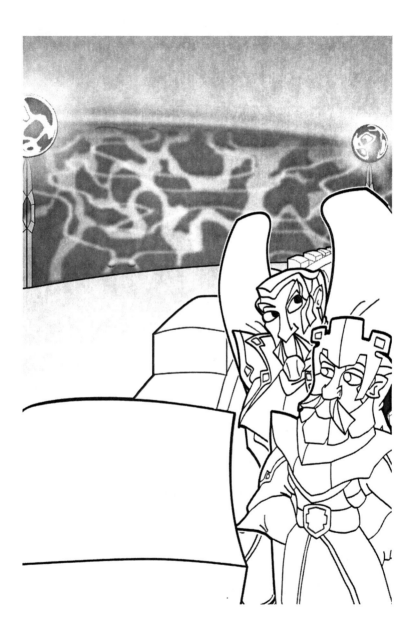

Marsonee was startled. "Is the boy ready?" he questioned. "Is he the one to fulfill the prophecy?"

"The Great Divide can no longer be allowed to stand," the King said. "The people must be reunited with their King."

"But if he is not ready...," Marsonee began.

"Only time can determine if the boy is ready," the King answered, stroking his short, white beard in thought. "We cannot force him to seek his destiny."

"And what of the Great Book, my King? Without it, there is no way to cross through the Great Divide. Only the Keeper can open the Book and reveal its wisdom. There has been no Keeper spawned in this generation."

"Every generation has produced a Keeper of the Book through the royal family of Devon. This generation has been no different," the King replied.

"The House of Devon has fallen to Flar and his armies of fire," Marsonee remarked. "King Devon has produced no heirs, save his daughter, and the Keeper has always been a male."

"Things are not always as they appear, Marsonee," the King answered. "Surely, you would know that as well as I. You must have faith that events will transpire in our favor. You must have faith in the people."

"What would you have me do then, my King?" Marsonee obediently asked.

"You will go to the village of Arter

and find the boy known as Justin. His parents will willingly give him to you. You will journey with Justin to the city of Rone. When you arrive there, you shall go to the ancient cathedral. In the catacombs, underneath the church, you both shall find who and what you are looking for."

"And you believe that this boy, Justin, can remove the sword from the stone cross?"

"Have you lost faith in the very prophecies that I have created?" the King asked.

Marsonee did not answer.

"When the boy does," the King continued, "the Golden Knight and his mighty order shall be reborn."

The King placed his hands on

9

Marsonee's shoulders. "Go now, my friend. May you find your faith again on your journey."

"I am your servant, my King," Marsonee replied, bowing slightly.

Marsonee walked to the edge of the castle wall. His mighty wings opened and began flapping swiftly. Marsonee rose upward and, within moments, he was flying toward the Great Divide.

 Chapter Two

Princess Rainna was led into the
throne room of Devon Castle by two
of the demonic fire soldiers of Flar.
In past times, the throne room was a
royal place, brightly decorated with the
sun colors of her parents, the king and
queen. Now, that elegance was gone. It
had been replaced by the dark, red and
black banners of Flar, the fire lord. As
she approached, Rainna saw Flar seated
on the bone and wood throne which once
belonged to her father as the head of the
House of Devon. Flar was an imposing
figure. When standing, he stood seven

feet tall. He was muscular in appearance. Flar was dressed in spiked armor with skulls on both shoulders. His eyes glowed with a red haze. Beside Flar, there stood the sorcerer.

Covered in dark robes, the sorcerer was slightly older than Rainna with a slim, frail body.

"Ah, Princess Rainna. How pleased I am that you could join us," Flar growled.

"You summoned me and I was given no choice," Rainna responded. She was young and very beautiful, her flowing dark hair only accented her deep, green eyes and tender lips.

"I believe you know my sorcerer, Murlox," Flar continued.

"I know only that his magic has

13

failed to open the Book," Rainna replied.

Flar stood, his long cape spreading onto the floor. He walked over to a long table and poured himself a drink. "There has been a need to make some changes at Devon Castle. Your father and mother have been placed into prison for their failure to reveal to me the identity of the Keeper."

"No!" Rainna cried. "They cannot reveal to you that which they do not know! Where have you placed them? I demand to know so I may see them!"

"You shall make no demands of me!" Flar roared. "You are a princess in name only now. Their dungeon is not a pleasant place. Perhaps you have some knowledge that you would like to share. Perhaps of a secret brother?"

"I know only of the prophecies," Rainna said. "And I know that I am an only child."

"That is impossible!" Flar screamed, slamming his fist against a stone column. "There is always a Keeper of the Book!"

"And where is the Book now?" Rainna asked. "It has been removed from the castle sanctuary."

"I can assure you, Princess, that the Book is safely in my care," Murlox said. "Here in the castle."

"I wish to see it," she said.

"You shall witness its destruction soon enough," Murlox replied.

"There is no power in this realm that can destroy the ancient Book," Rainna remarked. "No matter how many armies you bring, no matter how long you

oppress the people, there will come a time when the righteousness of the King will return to this land led by the courage of his Knights. You know it. You feel it. The time is coming. Soon."

"You should pray only that I do not grow tired of you," Flar snarled. "Away from me now, Princess."

"As you wish, Lord Flar," Rainna replied. She turned.

"You shall bow to your master!" Murlox ordered.

"I bow only to my King" Rainna replied. She was escorted out of the throne room by the two soldiers. After she had departed, Flar threw his cup against the stone wall, shattering it into pieces.

"Her defiance to us only grows," Flar angrily said. "What do your visions say?"

"What I see remains unclear,"

17

Murlox answered.

"You lie! You have seen the Golden Knight in your vision!" Flar snapped. "Do not play games with me, old man, or you will find a dungeon reserved for you!"

"What I have seen is foggy," Murlox calmly replied.

"Then see more clearly!" Flar roared. "Use your magic and destroy that worthless Book!"

"As you command, my lord." Murlox bowed as he backed away.

Flar stormed out of the throne room, knocking over two soldiers who attempted to open the large, wooden doors for him.

Chapter Three

Marsonee appeared in the skies over the farming village known as Arter. It was a small village, surrounded by fields on three sides and a large lake on the other. Marsonee immediately soared down to a modest, wooden hut held together by mud and straw. Inside, a woman sat knitting quietly while her husband stood shucking husks of corn.

"I have come for the boy named Justin," Marsonee said. "Are you not frightened by my presence?"

"I am not afraid," the woman replied, placing her yarn down. "So soon. Has the

time come so soon?"

"Great favor has been placed on this home," Marsonee remarked.

The man knelt down beside his wife and embraced her as gentle tears welled in their eyes.

"What does the King ask of us?" he said.

"Only the boy," Marsonee answered. "Where might he be found?"

"He is tending our fields," the man said. "I shall fetch him for you."

The man rose and left the house. Marsonee eyed the woman. She reached down and picked up her yarn. She began knitting again.

"You and your husband were not frightened by me," Marsonee remarked.

"Do you know of your son's destiny?"

"Yes," she answered, almost in a whisper. "I have known since the day of his birth."

"How can you know the mind of your King?"

A young boy, Justin, entered the house. He was followed by his father. When he saw Marsonee, Justin fell to his knees.

His mother rose from her chair and lovingly touched her son on the cheek.

"Do not be afraid, my child," she said. "Marsonee is here on behalf of the King and has come to take you with him. I shall prepare your things for the journey."

Justin slowly stood and watched as

his mother began packing clothes and things into a large, knapsack.

"You are older than I had imagined," Marsonee commented. "Not a boy, but not yet a man. When your mother has finished, we shall go."

"Where are you sending him?" his father asked.

"We go to the city of Rone," Marsonee replied.

"But...but I cannot leave my family now," Justin said. "The harvest is only weeks away and my father cannot do it alone. Flar already demands the village send so much corn and grain."

"My son," his father said, placing his hands on Justin's shoulders and looking deeply into his young, worried eyes. "Do not be concerned for your mother and me. There comes a time in every man's life when he must leave his family and seek his own way. You are not a farmer. Your path shall take you to greater things."

"But I cannot travel alone," Justin said.

"No one travels alone," his mother replied, placing the knapsack on the sole table, "when they travel in the service of their King."

"I will gather for you your horses," his father said. He left the house.

"We have no horses," Justin remarked. "Only mules for plowing."

"On that, we shall see," Marsonee said. "Come, let us go outside and see what your father has found for us."

25

They walked outside the house. Justin's father was leading two, beautiful stallions down the dirt pathway. Justin stared at the horses in amazement.

"How father?" Justin gasped, taking the rein and stroking the one horse on the side. "They are so strong."

"You have far to go and there are still several hours of daylight left," his father said. "You have no time to waste, my son."

Marsonee mounted one of the horses as Justin embraced his father and mother. Then, he too mounted a horse.

"I do not know why I am going," Justin said to his parents.

"Then go in faith," his mother replied. She looked at Marsonee. "Will I see him again?"

"Yes," Marsonee answered. "He will come back for you."

The archangel and the boy turned and rode way. His father and mother watched as the two figures slowly disappeared from view. She wiped a tear from her face.

"Are you sad?" her husband asked.

"No," she said with a slight laugh, turning to look into the distance at the Great Divide, "happy."

Chapter Four

Inside the dark chambers of the castle, the sorcerer, Murlox, had prepared to cast an evil spell in an attempt to destroy the Book. The room was dark and cold with the only light being provided by torches. Water seeped through the stone walls and trickled onto the floor. The room was also barren with just a grey, stone table resting in the middle. The Book sat on the table. It was large, perhaps several thousand pages, and on the cover was a large cross design. It was lined in gold, silver and bronze. Murlox was dressed in dark robes with images of the moon and demons laced in the cloth. He raised his frigid hands.

"I call upon the dark forces of the underworld to empower me with might of ancient evils to destroy this Book of Good!" Murlox screamed out. Streaks of energy began to form from the thin air and shoot across the room. "I feel your power, evil one. I feel your power to destroy!"

The wooden door creaked open and two fire guards pushed Princess Rainna into the room. Suddenly, a howling wind ripped through the chamber.

"Leave us," Murlox commanded. The two soldiers turned and left, slamming the door behind them. More flashes of energy exploded around them.

"What are you doing, Murlox?" Rainna yelled over the howling wind.

"I have summoned you here, Princess Rainna, to witness the destruction of your precious Book," Murlox retorted. "Ohla, bakor, demone, destroy!"

"You cannot harm the Book!" Rainna shouted. "No magic can harm it! It is of another realm!"

Then, the Book slowly rose from the table and hovered in mid-air. A white and yellow energy field appeared around it.

"Watch me, my helpless princess!"

Two beams of red and black energy shot from Murlox's hands. The beams struck the energy field surrounding the Book. There was a flash of white light and

the roar of an explosion. Murlox screamed in terror as he was thrown across the room. He crashed against the wall and sank to the floor.

Rainna was motionless despite the powerful wind which swept through her hair and dress. For a moment, she was blinded by the flash of light despite her attempt to cover her eyes. However, the wind and explosion did not knock her down. Then, as suddenly as it had all begun, all was silent and the wind was gone. She slowly opened her eyes. The Book rested quietly on the table, unharmed. Murlox struggled to his feet.

"How?" he mumbled. "How could it survive such power?"

"Your black magic is no equal to the

wisdom of the Book," Rainna remarked. "If there is nothing else..."

"Do not speak to me," Murlox barked, shoving his wrinkled finger in her face. "Guards!"

The two fire soldiers entered the chamber.

"Take Princess Rainna back to her room," he commanded them.

The guards approached her. They grabbed her by the arms. She struggled for a moment before they began to drag her out.

"Wait," Murlox said. He walked over to her and ran his pale hand across her cheek. "You are young and foolish, Princess. You cling to a false hope that an ancient prophecy will be fulfilled. So

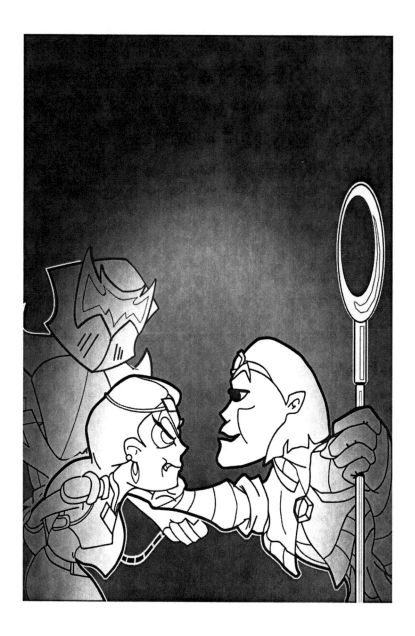

the Book survives another night. How long before the Keeper is revealed and brought before us? Look around you, little girl. There is nothing for you. The House of Devon exists only to serve Lord Flar. Soon, even Flar will have no further use for you. Unless you become mine, there is no hope for you."

"There is always hope," Rainna defiantly answered.

"We shall see," Murlox replied with a crooked smile. He waved the guards to remove her. As Rainna disappeared and the chamber door slammed shut, Murlox turned and gazed fiendishly at the Book resting silently on the stone table.

The fire guards led Rainna up the stairs of one of the castle's towers. They shoved her into her bedroom, locked the door and left. She looked around sadly. It was a simple room with only a worn bed of straw, a wooden table and a cracked mirror. It was hardly what one would expect for a royal princess. Rainna walked over to her bed and fell to her knees. Placing her head in her hands, she wept.

"When? When, my King, shall you deliver us?" she called out into the darkness. She rose from the floor.

Rainna looked at the jewels and rings on her fingers. She took them off and threw them across the room.

"They are nothing," she cried. "All the riches of this land are nothing without my King!"

Rainna wept again.

Suddenly, a gentle breeze of wind rushed through her hair. It was soothing

and cool. Rainna reached up to try and touch it, but she could not. She looked around quickly and saw a figure standing there in the darkness.

"Who are you?" she called out.

"Do not approach me," the figure said. It was a young girl's voice. "Take the Book to the city of Rone. Your King has heard you, Rainna. Your horse is ready. Speak of my instructions to no one."

There was another gush of wind and the figure was gone. Rainna looked down at her hands. The rings and jewels had been returned.

Chapter Five

They rode together, Marsonee and Justin, on the road to Rone. It was late evening and the sun was beginning to set on the horizon.

"Will I get to see the King?" Justin asked. "Is he in Rone?"

"In time, all people will see the King," Marsonee answered. "But, he is not in Rone. The King lives beyond the Great Divide in the Kingdom."

"Are we supposed to worship him?"

"The King is wise and just. We must be obedient to him. All things exist through the King. In turn, he gives us freedom."

"Why does Flar not allow the people to speak of the King?" Justin asked.

"He fears the great power of the King," Marsonee answered. "He knows that if given the choice, the people would choose the King over him."

"And the Golden Knight, who is he?"

"Hmm...," Marsonee chuckled. "Has it been so long that this generation has forgotten the tales of the Golden Knight and his Holy Order?"

"There is more than one knight?" Justin excitedly asked.

"Oh, yes, there is more than one knight," Marsonee replied. "There are twelve knights in all, but the Golden Knight has been chosen by the King to be their leader. Many generations ago, long before your parents even walked this land, the King lived among your people and ruled over them. The Knights of the Holy Order were his champions and the protector of the people. No evil was allowed to form in the Kingdom before the knights would seek it out and destroy it."

"What happened to them?"

"As with all things, the people eventually turned away from their heroes," Marsonee sighed.

"And the King believes that I may be the Golden Knight?" Justin asked.

"Only time will tell, my young boy," Marsonee replied. "That answer is not for me to know. Just the King can truly know your destiny."

"You have doubts," Justin said. "I can tell that, you know. You don't believe that I could be the Golden Knight."

Marsonee stared at him intently.

"There are great trials ahead for the Golden Knight and for this kingdom," he said. "If you are to be him, I pray that you will be equal to the task before us."

"You are very serious to be an angel," Justin said. "You do know that, Marsonee."

"And what makes you think that I am an angel?" Marsonee asked.

Justin pointed at Marsonee's back. "The wings. I mean, they give it away."

"They can be quite useful."

"I like the wings," Justin commented. "They really add something."

"I am an archangel," Marsonee said. "We are a higher order of the angels. And we are always very serious beings."

"Can you tell me more about the Golden Knight?" Justin asked. "I want to know everything."

THE BOY IS SUMMONED

"In time, Justin. In time," Marsonee halted his horse. "It will be dark soon and the roads will not be safe for travel. There is a clearing up ahead. We will camp there for the night."

"If you're an archangel," Justin said. "surely a bunch of robbers doesn't frighten you."

"It is not for me that I am fearful," Marsonee replied. "You have no weapon and I have pledged to my King to see you safely to Rone. We have journeyed far today. Rest will do you good."

"I will be the Golden Knight," Justin forcefully said. "I will protect the King."

"To be the Golden Knight, my boy, one must put the protection of others before thy very self."

Chapter Six

Princess Rainna rose from her bed and wrapped herself in a hooded cloak. There was a clap of thunder and a flash of lightning outside her window. Gazing through the metal bars, she could see a storm brewing over the castle. She walked to the bedroom door and pushed. It was locked. Taking a small hair pin from her mirror stand, Rainna began trying to pick the lock.

"Do not fail me now," she mumbled to herself.

After several attempts, the door creaked open. She looked down the hallway. It was empty. Rainna slowly and carefully began creeping down the stone stairwell toward the castle's inner chambers.

As she made her way down, Rainna could hear the columns of soldiers marching about the castle. She pulled the hood over her face and avoided making any eye contact with them. Within minutes, she had reached the sorcerer's chamber undetected.

The room was dark and hauntingly quiet when she entered. In the center of the room, the Book rested on the table. Rainna removed the hood from her face. As she approached, Rainna could not help but be awed by its peaceful beauty. She lifted it off the table with relative ease despite its size. She traced the cross design on the cover with her finger.

"You will be safe," she whispered. "I will keep you safe."

"A little late for a stroll, don't you think Princess?" Murlox said.

Rainna turned quickly and saw the sorcerer standing in the doorway with two fire soldiers.

"I'm taking the Book to a safer place," Rainna remarked. "Away from you and Flar."

"I can assure you, there is no place better for that book than Devon Castle," Murlox answered. "Now be a wise girl and return it to the table."

"I don't think so."

"As you wish then," Murlox slyly said. "Seize her."

The fire soldiers stepped forward. Rainna stumbled backwards until she finally struck the wall. Suddenly, there was a blinding flash of light which filled the entire chamber.

"Aaahhh!" Murlox grimaced in pain

as he tried vainly to cover his eyes. As he recovered his sight, Murlox quickly shot glances around the room. All that remained was himself and the two fire soldiers. Rainna and the Book were gone.

"Don't just stand there!" Murlox gasped in amazement. "After her!"

Rainna raced down the hallway. Up ahead, she could hear the sound of approaching soldiers. Looking around quickly, she noticed another staircase.

"There she is!" Murlox cried, directly behind her. "Do not let her escape!"

Realizing there was nowhere to go but up, Rainna bolted up the stairs. They seemed to go on forever. She knew she could not stop as she could hear the sound of the soldiers behind her. Finally reaching the top, she swung open the wooden door and ran out onto the castle ramparts. The storm was in full force now with rain pouring down and lightning streaking across the sky. Rainna looked around frantically as she found to her dismay that she was trapped.

"What do I do now?" she whispered, gasping for breath. "I cannot fail my King. I cannot fail the Book."

Murlox and the fire soldiers appeared in the doorway.

"Wonderful weather we're having, isn't it?" Murlox sarcastically remarked.

"Not one step further or I'll..." Rainna shouted as she lifted the Book over her head.

"Or you'll do what, Princess?" Murlox heckled. "Go ahead and throw it over the wall and into the moat. We will simply retrieve it from the waters in the morning."

Rainna looked over the castle wall

in panic. In amazement, directly below, she could see her horse waiting, prancing in panic as a bolt of lightning flashed overhead, followed by a clap of thunder.

"You're trapped, Rainna," Murlox continued. "There is nowhere left for you to go. Surrender to me now and I will recommend a lighter punishment for you to Lord Flar."

"No, I will not surrender! I will be your prisoner no longer, Murlox!" Rainna cried. She climbed onto the top of the wall. She could feel the rain streaming down her face.

"Very well then," Murlox said. He motioned to the two fire soldiers. "I had grown tired of you, Princess, long ago."

The demonic soldiers drew their swords. The blades immediately engulfed themselves in flames. They approached her

53

with devilish grins on their skeletal faces.
As they drew near, one of the soldiers raised
his blazing sword to strike her.

"No," Rainna almost whispered as
she closed her eyes to accept her fate.
She clutched the Book firmly against her
chest. It began to glow.

An arrow streaked through the night
sky and struck the fire soldier squarely
in the face. He toppled backwards and
collapsed to the ground.

"How?" Rainna gasped as she wiped
a strand of hair from her face. She rose
and gazed out into the stormy night.
There, perhaps fifty or sixty yards away,
a figure in white robes, basked in radiant
light, hovered in the air supported by the
flapping of his mighty wings. He held a
bow in his hands with a quiver of arrows
strapped to his back. He removed another

arrow and reloaded the bow. With ease, he pulled the bowstring back.

"Get down! Get down, you fool!" Murlox screamed to the remaining fire soldier.

The second arrow struck the fire soldier in the shoulder. He arched back in pain and stumbled backwards, dropping his sword to the ground.

"Step off, Rainna!" the figure commanded.

"But, I'll fall!" Rainna cried back.

"Where is thy faith? Step off!"

Rainna reached down and grabbed the fire soldier's sword. She closed her eyes and stepped off the castle wall into the darkness. To her surprise, she did not fall. Rainna opened her eyes and saw a small, yellow, cushion of energy had formed underneath her feet. Despite the

storm, it lowered her slowly and safely to the ground below and then vanished. The Book was no longer glowing. Rainna carefully placed it in her saddlebag.

As she calmed and mounted her giddy horse, she looked up into the night sky to see if her rescuer was still there. To her surprise once again, the figure was gone. Rainna nudged her horse and galloped quickly away through the storm.

Murlox rushed to the castle wall in time to see the princess riding away. The wounded fire soldier stood, the arrow still in his shoulder.

"Speak of this to no one," Murlox said, brushing the soldier aside. "I know where she is going."

Chapter Seven

Justin and Marsonee sat around a campfire. Both of them held a stick with a piece of meat on it over the fire. The horses were tied to a nearby tree and a small, makeshift tent made of burlap had been put together.

"It's hard to imagine an archangel needing to eat," Justin said, taking a bite of his meat. "Or being such a good cook."

"In your world, we must do as you do," Marsonee replied. "Including sleep."

"How many archangels are there?" Justin asked. "A couple hundred, maybe?"

Marsonee chuckled and looked up into the night. "No, my boy. Not a hundred. We are as numerous as the stars you see in the sky."

"There's too many stars to even count," Justin remarked. "Have you been in many battles?"

"Oh yes, far too many battles," Marsonee reflected. "Far too many comrades lost. But, as long as evil makes war on the good, we will stand ready."

"Can an archangel die?"

"Yes, but not in the sense of your level of understanding," Marsonee said, taking a bite. "Hmm...still slightly undercooked."

"Will you train me," Justin asked, "so I can be a great warrior?"

"No training will be required from me," Marsonee replied. "Many things you already know. The rest will be revealed to you in the Book."

"The Book?" Justin questioned.

"The Book contains the laws of the King," Marsonee answered. "It is a guide to the Kingdom. Only through the Book can the Great Divide be crossed."

"Is it the source of a knight's power?"

"No," Marsonee said. "All of a knight's power and virtue flows from the King. And powerful, a knight will be. The Book is merely a gateway to the Kingdom."

"Is the Book in Rone?"

"Unfortunately, my boy, it is not. The Book is in the hands of Flar, the fire lord, who now commands Castle Devon. That is why we must move quickly. If Flar was to discover who is the Keeper of the Book and destroy him, all would be lost."

"If the Book is not in Rone, then why do we go there?"

"Because that is what I was instructed to do," Marsonee said.

"You speak in such riddles, Marsonee," Justin said. "I feel as if I will never understand."

"Prophecy is never easy to understand," the archangel answered. "But your willingness to learn and act on faith that what I am telling you is true is encouraging to me."

They sat in silence for several moments.

"Do you know of Princess Rainna?" Justin finally asked.

"I know she is of the House of

Devon."

"She came to Arter once," Justin said. "And I saw her. My parents say she does not agree with the rulings of Flar."

"Did she see you?" Marsonee questioned.

"No, I don't think so. When her carriage was coming through the village, she dropped one of her rings on the ground and I picked it up. I keep it with me, just in case I ever see her again. It's been like a good luck charm for me."

Justin stood up from the fire and walked over to his horse. He rummaged through his saddlebag.

"I have found that no charm can give one luck," Marsonee said.

"Here it is," Justin remarked. He

tossed it across the clearing to Marsonee who caught it with his large hand. It was a beautiful ring with a large cross in the center. The cross was surrounded with gold, silver and bronze. "You would think she would have come back to get it."

"And this ring came from the finger of Princess Rainna?" Marsonee asked.

"It did," Justin said. "I will never forget it. She was so beautiful."

"Devon Castle is far from here. I doubt that you will ever see her again," Marsonee said. "Perhaps it is best if I hold onto this ring for now. Go and rest. I will take the first watch."

"It looks like storm clouds to the east," Justin said. "Do you think it will rain tomorrow?"

"I see the dark clouds that you speak of. But, they are far off. The sky is clear now."

"Good night, Marsonee."

"Good night, my boy, and do not be troubled."

Justin crouched down and pushed the tent flap aside. He stared at the mighty archangel sitting sadly alone by the fire. Justin crawled into the tent and went to sleep.

Marsonee examined the ring again.

"I have seen this ring before," he whispered to himself, "but I cannot recall where."

Several hours passed. Marsonee rose and walked over to a small pile of wood. He collected several pieces and placed them on the fire.

Suddenly, the night was shattered by a scream.

To Be Continued…

The Adventure continues in *The Golden Knight #2: The Battle for Rone!* Coming Soon!

About the Authors and Illustrator

It all started when a 12 year old boy asked his father a simple question: "Dad, can you help me write a story for these characters that I created?" A few months would pass before the world of the Golden Knight was born. **Justin Clark** is a student at Cass Middle School and a member of its Art Club. Justin loves anime and superheroes. He draws and creates many of his own characters. His father, **Steven Clark**, has written stories, songs, stage plays and poems since high school. He is a graduate of Kennesaw State University with a degree in history. The Clark family (Steven, Leslie, Justin, Jason and Brooke) live in Georgia.

It was fate or sheer luck that brought **Taylor Gibson** and Steven and Justin Clark together. After responding to an online advertisement for an illustrator, Taylor was chosen out of a number of candidates to be the artist for The Golden Knight. With experience in graphic design and manga style artwork, Taylor was the perfect person to take Justin's sketches and characters and bring them to life. Taylor lives in North Carolina.